BATTLE AGAINST THE
BLACK ORDER

MARVEL

CRRAACK!

A massive sound jolted through Avengers Tower, where Shuri and T'Challa were showing Doctor Bruce Banner some Wakandan tech they were working on.

"What was that?" Shuri asked.

"It wasn't thunder, that's for sure," said Banner. "Let's check it out."

"Proxima Midnight!"

Banner had heard tales of the Super Villain, one of Thanos's strongest allies, throughout the years. "What is she doing on Earth?"

"Give me a hand and I'll explain later!" Captain Marvel called out. Give her a hand? Shuri couldn't! Her gauntlets weren't ready yet!

Shuri ran back to the lab in Avengers Tower to fix her gauntlets.
Banner turned into the Hulk and followed T'Challa into the fight.
WHACK! Proxima immediately attacked Black Panther.

Hulk knocked Proxima Midnight into the sky—right toward the edge of the roof!

"Hulk smash!" Black Panther called out. He looked excited. "I've always wanted to say that."

Captain Marvel needed to find out what Proxima was doing on Earth in the
first place. But before Captain Marvel could reach her,

Proxima Midnight disappeared!

"There were two members of the Black Order coming to Earth: Proxima and Corvus Glaive," Captain Marvel said.

"Why do you think they're here?" Black Panther asked.

Captain Marvel shook her head. "All I know is that if Thanos sent them, they're up to no good."

"Banner! Help!" Suddenly, Banner got an incoming distress call from Ant-Ma

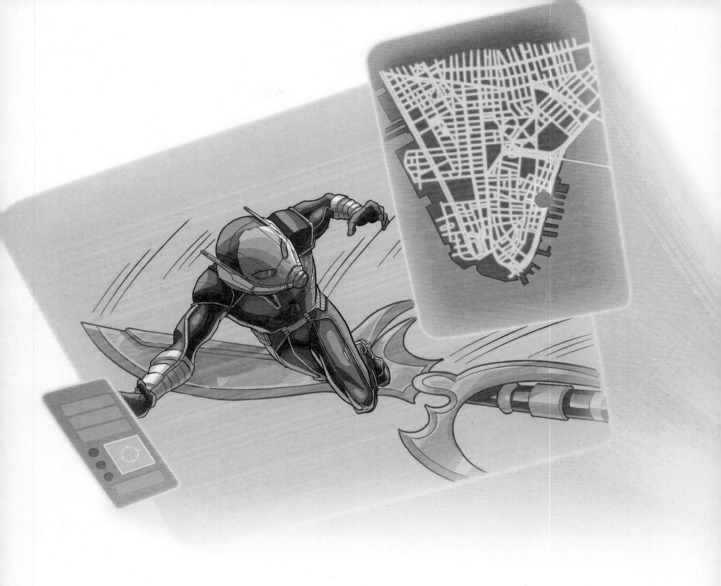

"That's Corvus Glaive's weapon," Captain Marvel said urgently, watching the tiny hero dodge and dash away from the glinting blade.

"Look," Banner said, pointing at the map. "We have to get to the waterfront!"

"I'll catch up!" Shuri called from the lab. "Soon as I get these gauntlets working..."

"Hurry, sister!" Black Panther urged her on.

"Boy, am I glad to see you guys!" Ant-Man heralded the arriving Avengers. "Who is this guy?"

Captain Marvel blasted Corvus. "Corvus Glaive," she said. "One of Thanos's pawns. What I don't know is why he's after you."

"I can answer that," Corvus said. "Thanos wants Ant-Man because he wants to know how Pym Particles work."

The Avengers shared a grimace. Pym Particles were responsible for giving Ant-Man his powers to grow and shrink.

n the hands of Thanos, the particles could be catastrophic!

"Well, Thanos isn't finding that out today," Captain Marvel said. Black Panther nodded. "You fight one of us, you fight all of us."

"I don't care," Corvus Glaive said dismissively. "What Thanos wants, Thanos gets!"

BAM!

Black Panther landed a surprise kick, bringing Corvus to his knees, at which point Captain Marvel discharged a knockout blow.

"That's what I call a one-two punch," she said, giving Black Panther a high five.

But just as Hulk was about to deliver the finishing touch . . .

Proxima Midnight reappeared!

"Oh geez," Ant-Man said in disbelief. "There's another one?!"

"You were barely able to handle one of us," Proxima gloated. "How can you fight us both?"

"I was wondering that myself," Ant-Man said, as the rest of the heroes gathered to protect him. Without the whole team in place,

the heroes had their hands full!

Black Panther sailed toward Captain Marvel after a rough blow from Corvus. "I feel like we could really use Shuri and those new-and-improved blasters right about now," Captain Marvel said.

"Um . . . guys? Over here?" Ant-Man gave a nervous chuckle as he struggled against Proxima. Any moment, she would teleport away with him, and Thanos would have the secret of Pym Particles.

How could the heroes stop them?

POW!

Shuri appeared out of nowhere and knocked Proxima flying with an energy punch from her updated gauntlets. Ant-Man was set free! "She hits like the Hulk!" Captain Marvel said.

With Shuri's tech, the Super Heroes quickly gained the upper hand.
"Better late than never!" Black Panther called out to his sister. Shuri laughed.
"The combination of Wakandan and Stark tech is unbeatable!"
Proxima and Corvus teleported away.

"Whew," Ant-Man said. "That was too close."

"Piece of cake," Shuri said. "All we had to do was get the whole team together."

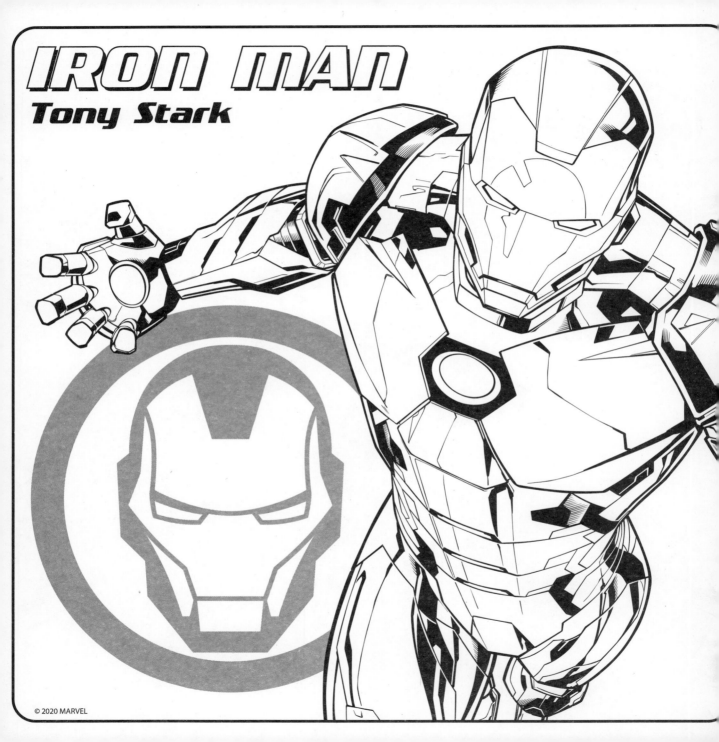

© 2020 MARVEL

BLACK WIDOW
Natasha Romanoff

ULTRON

VISION

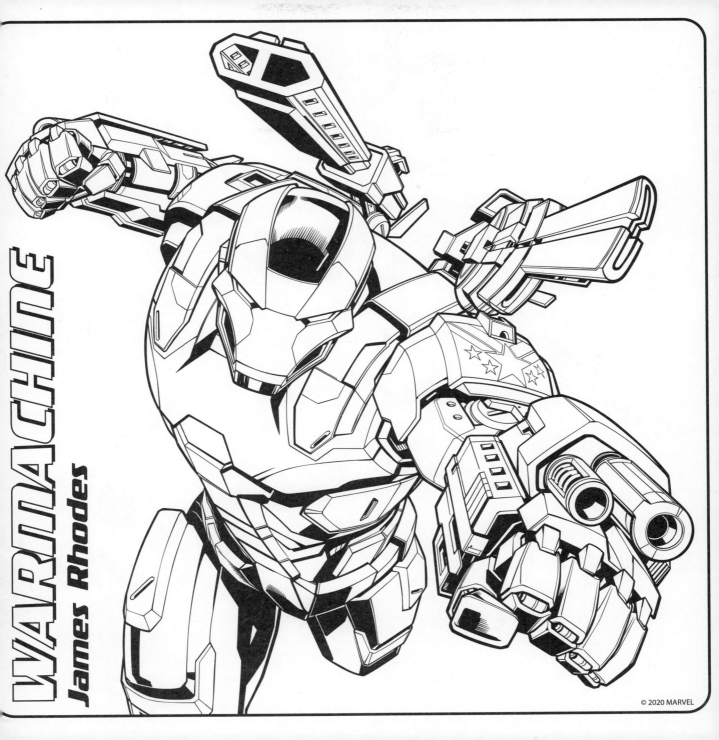

WARMACHINE

James Rhodes

© 2020 MARVEL

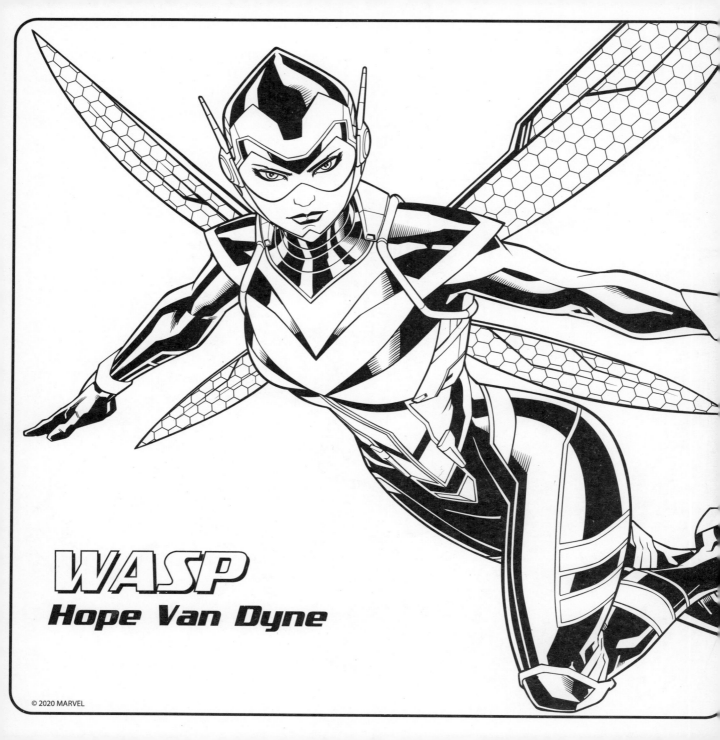

WASP
Hope Van Dyne

THOR
Thor Odinson

© 2020 MARVEL

DOCTOR STRANGE
Dr. Stephen Strange

RED SKULL

© 2020 MARVEL

FALCON
Sam Wilson

© 2020 MARVEL

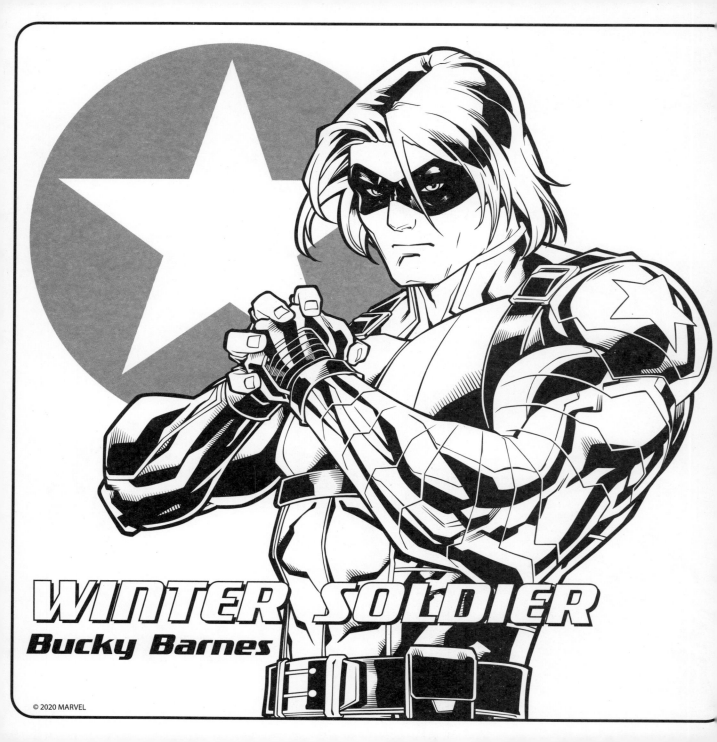

WINTER SOLDIER
Bucky Barnes

BLACK PANTHER
King T'Challa